Oscar Fay Adams

# A Motley Jest

Salzwasser

**Oscar Fay Adams**

# A Motley Jest

1. Auflage | ISBN: 978-3-84604-750-7

Erscheinungsort: Frankfurt, Deutschland

Erscheinungsjahr: 2020

Salzwasser Verlag GmbH

Reprint of the original, first published in 1909.

# A Motley Jest

## SHAKESPEAREAN DIVERSIONS

## By Oscar Fay Adams

AUTHOR OF "A DICTIONARY OF AMERICAN AUTHORS," "THE
STORY OF JANE AUSTEN'S LIFE," "SICUT PATRIBUS
AND OTHER VERSE," ETC.; AMERICAN EDITOR
OF THE HENRY IRVING SHAKESPEARE,

ETC.

LEGE
QUID
LEGAS

BOSTON

Sherman, French & Company

1909

TO THE

OLD CAMBRIDGE SHAKESPEARE ASSOCIATION

THIS

LITTLE VOLUME

IS

GRATEFULLY INSCRIBED

## PREFATORY NOTE

The Sixth Act of *The Merchant of Venice* was first printed in the *Cornhill Booklet* for March, 1903. The *Shakespearean Fantasy* now appears for the first time in print.

# CONTENTS

# I

# A SHAKESPEAREAN FANTASY

# A SHAKESPEAREAN FANTASY

## SCENE I.

*An island in the Middle Seas. A cave is seen on the right and before it, under a palm tree, CALIBAN is discovered sleeping.*

*Enter TRINCULO and STEPHANO, quarreling.*

TRINCULO. Since the day when the old gentleman they call Prospero took it into his bald pate to disappear into air along with a most goodly company beside, there's not a bottle to be found i' this isle, as I am a good Christian, and, what is more, a good Christian man's son.

STEPHANO. Bottle me no bottles, Trinculo. Had we ne'er shared a bottle betwixt us we had not been left to bide by ourselves in this whoreson isle in the hard service of the man-monster, Caliban, but might be in fair Naples at this very hour.

TRINCULO. Sagely said, Master Stephano. Thou wast ever wise enow i' the tail o' the event. An' thou could'st have looked it thus wisely i' the mouth, thou hadst been a made man, Stephano, a made man, and a householder, to boot.

[ 1 ]

STEPHANO. By mine head, a scurvy trick o' the King to give us over to a dog's life in this heathen isle with a man-monster for a master, and none other company beside.

TRINCULO. More wisdom from that mouth of thine, most sage Stephano. Thou art indeed become a second Socrates for sober conclusions.

CALIBAN [*awaking*] What, Trinculo! Get me some food, I say, or thy bones shall pay thy jape. Get thee hence at once, for a mighty hunger is come upon me and I would eat. [*To* STEPHANO] Sing thou, and caper nimbly the while.

STEPHANO [*sings and dances clumsily*]

> A lass I had,
> A lass I had,
> But I've a lass no longer.
> She's dead and cold
> In churchyard mould
> Grim Death he was the stronger.

ARIEL [*invisible*] *sings.*

> In churchyard mould
> She lieth cold:
> From her dust the violets spring.

[ 2 ]

To her dark bed
Have fairies sped
To sing her welcoming.

CALIBAN [*alarmed*]   Methinks like music have
    I heard before
When Prospero I did serve.   And it should bode
Damn'd Prospero's return then were I slave
Again, doing his will in everything.

STEPHANO.   What is this same that sings i' the
air without lips or body?

TRINCULO [*returning with food which he places
before* CALIBAN]   Master Nobody is at his ancient tricks.   An' he be a devil, he hath an angel's
voice.

CALIBAN.   Retire ye both, for I would be alone.
              [*Exeunt* TRINCULO *and* STEPHANO.
ARIEL *plays softly on a tabor, scatters poppy
leaves and departs, leaving* CALIBAN *asleep.*

## SCENE II.

*A room in the palace at Naples.*

*Enter* FERDINAND *and* MIRANDA.

FERDINAND.  Admir'd Miranda, you are sad,
and sad
Am I you should be sad.  Then will you not
Declare what canker eats your tender rose
That I may kill 't, or what untoward care
Weighs down your spirit, that I may kiss 't away?
   MIRANDA.  O, my sweet prince, my husband
      Ferdinand,
In truth I am not well, and yet I am,
And yet again I am not.  What say I?
It is no fever of the blood, no pain
That speaks in sharp besetment which doth ail
Me now.  Not these, and yet 'tis somewhat, still,
And when I bid it down 't will not away.
   FERDINAND.  O lov'd Miranda, ope thy soul to
      me.
   MIRANDA.  'Tis silly, sooth, too simple for
      your ear
To heed 't, and I unworthy of your love
To waste a single thought on it.  O teach
Me to forget it utterly.

FERDINAND.                    O sweet,
And so I will, when I do know what is 't
Thou would'st forget.
    MIRANDA.            And will you then forgive?
    FERDINAND.  I will, and yet I'm sure it is no
        fault
Needing forgiveness.
    MIRANDA.            You shall hear.  In brief,
Since you will have the truth, I fain would see
Once more that isle where I beheld you first.
Might I behold it once again and but
For once, I then were satisfied, so you
Were by my side beholding it likewise.
    FERDINAND.  Would I might bear thee hence
        within this hour,
For that dear isle I love because of thee.
But our philosophers declare the spot
Was but enchantment rais'd by wizard spells
And sunk in ocean's maw when Prospero,
Thy father, will'd it; never yet laid down
Good solid earth and rock on mortal map
And chart.  How this may be I know not, yet
Our sailors swear that no such isle there is
And truly they should know their own realm best.
    MIRANDA.  I'm sure 't was no enchantment.
    FERDINAND.                    Save the maid

Who dwelt upon 't, for she did cast a spell
About me when these eyes did first behold
Her there, and naught can take 't away.
    MIRANDA.                     Nay, now,
      You jest, sweet sir.
    FERDINAND.        No jest, I swear to thee.
    ARIEL [*sings*]

> Where, O where,
> Is the isle so fair?
> 'Tis far to the east,
> 'Tis far to the west;
> 'Tis here, 'tis there,
> That isle so fair:
> O where, O where?
> 'Tis everywhere,
> That isle so fair.

    MIRANDA. 'Tis Ariel's voice, my Ferdinand,
      but whence —                 [*sleeps.*
    FERDINAND [*drowsily*] The voice we heard
      upon the isle long since.
Sweet sound, with poppies curiously mix'd —
                             [*sleeps.*

### Scene III.

*The island in the Middle Seas.*

Ferdinand *and* Miranda *discovered sleeping on
a grassy mound. Soft music heard.*

Ferdinand [*awaking*]   With poppies mix'd —
O, I did dream — but where
Am I? 'Tis strange, and yet not strange.  This
   place
I do remember.  Here Miranda saw
I first —
Miranda [*awaking*]
         How say you, husband, I have slept,
And all I look no now is chang'd, and yet
Not so, for surely here I dwelt of old
With Prospero, my father.
Ferdinand.               'Tis naught else
But the same place, and we transported hence
Perchance as playthings of some kindly god,
Hearing thy tale and loving thee.
Miranda.                        Sweet prince,
My Ferdinand, then do we wake indeed,
Or is't enchantment, and a sleep?
Ferdinand.                     I deem
It truth, and be it thus, or not, in truth

[ 7 ]

'Tis pleasant seeming, and we twain will fleet
The time as happily as when each knew
The other first.  [CALIBAN *approaches, groveling*
 CALIBAN [*aside*]  O Setebos, 'tis she,
Damn'd Prospero's daughter.— Mistress, if it be
Thou'rt come to rule the isle I'll serve thee well,
And Prospero be absent.  Him I fear
As I do dread the awesome thunderstone.
 FERDINAND.  Lo! here come other of his company.
     TRINCULO *and* STEPHANO *approach.*
 TRINCULO.  Behold us, gentles, two as unhappy wights as ever 'scaped a hanging, or death by attorney.
 STEPHANO.  He speaks very true, as 't were, now and then, and we two honest men from Naples be now in most wretched case — slaves to the man-monster, Caliban.
  *Thunder heard.* CALIBAN, STEPHANO *and* TRINCULO *disperse by several ways and* FERDINAND *and* MIRANDA *retire to a cave near by.*

## Scene IV.

*Another part of the same.*

*Enter* Prospero.

Prospero.  My charms yet hold, though long
    disus'd, for I
Pitying Miranda's melancholy plight
By magic of mine art have hither brought
Duke Ferdinand and her that so the twain
Belov'd may live their first joys o'er again.
Here shall they speed the time a full month's space,
In such wise as they list, and then, at whiles,
Will I for their beguilement cause to pass
Before their eyes, when they shall sit at ease,
Weary of wandering o'er the mazy isle,
Figures of men and women, such, forsooth,
As Master Shakescene writ of in his plays.
These in their habit as they liv'd in those
Same plays I'll re-create for their delight,
Peopling a mimic world with mimic folk,
And making so this desert populous.    [*Exit.*

[9]

## Scene V.

*Another part of the same.*

*A grassy space shaded by palms, before a cave at whose entrance* FERDINAND *and* MIRANDA *are discovered playing chess.*

MIRANDA. O Ferdinand, the play was mine.

FERDINAND.                                     I thought
'Twas mine, but it shall e'en be as you will;
I'll take it back.

MIRANDA.          Indeed, you should not, prince,
For whatso'er you do it seemeth right
To me, and now I see I did mistake.
Good sooth, I will not have it back. I say,
I will not have it back — but what are these
Tending their steps this way? a halting pair.

                                    *Enter* NURSE *and* PETER.

NURSE. Peter!

PETER. Anon.

NURSE. Take my cloak, Peter. Truly the sun's heat hath made me all of a quiver, as they say. Marry I would e'en taste a little food before I go a step more. I'll warrant you we are many a mile from Verona by this.

PETER. A good mile, I take it, for I was never in this place before that I wot of.

NURSE. Say'st thou so, Peter?

PETER. Marry, that do I, and will answer to 't before any of womankind, and any of mankind too, that be less lusty than I.

NURSE. Peter!

PETER. Anon.

NURSE. Some food, Peter, and presently.

PETER. Here be strange fruits whose use I know not. A serving man of the young county Paris's did to my knowing eat an apple that was brought from afar in a ship's stomach, being a lusty youth and tall and much given to victual, and he did swell to bursting and died thereof while one might count thirteen by the clock. He made a fearsome dead body, as the saying is.

NURSE. Peter.

PETER. Anon.

NURSE. Thou shalt taste these fruits for me singly and in order, good Peter, and if no such harm come to thee as thou pratest of, then will I eat likewise.

PETER. Nay, but nurse, good nurse, good lady nurse —

NURSE. Hold thy peace, thou scurvy knave.

Would'st suffer me to go nigh to death for lack of food and thou stand by the while like a jack o' the clock when his hour has struck? Out upon thee, and do my pleasure quickly.

*Enter* MERCUTIO *and* ROMEO.

MERCUTIO. Here's fine matter toward. Thy Juliet's nurse, and her man Peter, quarrelling.

NURSE. God ye good den, gentlemen.

MERCUTIO. God ye good morrow, most ancient, and most fair ancient lady. Thy five wits, meseems, are gone far astray the whiles.

NURSE. Is it but good morrow? I had sworn 'twere long past noon, but, indeed, in this strange place, as one may say, there's no telling so simple a circumstance as the time of day.

ROMEO. Many things there be of which there's no telling, such as the number of times a maid will say no, when her mind is to say yes; how many days the wind will sit i' the east when one would desire fair weather; and how many years the toothless grandsire will wither out a young man's revenue.

NURSE. That is all very wisely said, good sir. Are you that he they call the young Romeo?

MERCUTIO. He is rightly called Romeo, but as for his youth, if knavery be not left out of the count, why then was Methusaleh a very babe to him, a suckling babe.

Nurse. Say you so? Then will I tell my lady Juliet so much, an' I can come by her in this heathen place.

Mercutio. Most ancient lady, yon Romeo would deceive the devil himself.

Nurse. Beshrew my heart. Then were my young mistress (who, to be sure, is no kind of a devil at all, saving your presences), led straight to a fool's paradise. She shall know, and presently, what a piece of man he is.

Mercutio [*seeing* Miranda *and* Ferdinand.
O Romeo the young; young Romeo,
Forget thy Juliet but a space, for here
A lady is, fairer than Juliet, [*pointing to* Mi-
    randa]
And mine eyes serve me truly.

Romeo.                    O how rare
One pearl's esteem'd until another's found,
While that becomes the chief, till straight a third
Shines forth. So is't with me. When Rosaline
I saw no lesser she might then with her
Compare. Next Juliet came athwart my sight,
And her I lov'd, forgetting Rosaline.
But now is Capulet's young daughter sped

From forth my heart and in her place this fair
Unknown in Juliet's stead is worshipped.

> *He seems about to approach* MIRANDA, *but
> is withheld by* MERCUTIO.

MERCUTIO. Inconstant Romeo, have a care.
　　For me,
I think her wed, and that the husband there,
May have a word to change with thee.

ROMEO.　　　　　　　　　　　　Prate not
To me of husbands, my Mercutio —

MERCUTIO. Have peace, rash Romeo, thou —
　　But who comes here?

> *Enter* OPHELIA, *strewing flowers.*

Poor, tearful lady! See, she weeps, and smiles
Aweeping, wrings her hand, and smiles again.

ROMEO. She makes as if to speak to us, poor
　　soul,

OPHELIA. This is All Hallow Eve. They say
to-night each Jill may see her Jack that is to
come. But these be idle tales to juggle us poor
maids, withal, for I no Jack have found. Cophetua, they say, was a king who was wed to a beggar
maid; a pretty tale is't not? But there's no truth
in't; there be no such happenings now, for my
love was a prince indeed, but we were never wed, and
now he is gone. [*Weeps*] He was a goodly

youth to look on, but he is dead by this and burns in hell.  [*Sings*]

He is dead who wronged the maid;
 He is dead, perdy.
In the grave his bones are laid,
 Hey, and woe is me.

O my love was tall and fine;
 Fair he was to see.
As light doth from a jewel shine,
 His eyes shined on me.

I cry your pardon, good people all.  But there's something lost, I think, and 't will not be found for all my searching.

*Enter* HAMLET.

HAMLET.  The fair Ophelia.  Sweet maid, do you not know me?

OPHELIA.  No, forsooth; I did never see you before, and yet methinks your eye hath a trick of Prince Hamlet's in it.  But that's all one, for the Lord Hamlet is dead, and they say his soul is in hell for cozening us poor maids.  [*Sings*]

He is dead that wronged the maid;
 He is dead, perdy.

[ 15 ]

MIRANDA. I scarce can see for weeping. Would there were
But somewhat I might do to ease her pain.
    FERDINAND. Her woe, me thinketh, is long past its cure.
But look! here comes a sadder wight than she.

        *Enter* CONSTANCE, *with hair unbound.*

    CONSTANCE [*to* OPHELIA] Thy wits are all disorder'd as mine own:
Then might we play at grief as who should know
The worst, but mine's the heavier. You do mourn
A lover faithless, I a son whose face,
So sweet and gracious, made the world for me;
Perpetual solace to my widowhood.

    OPHELIA. I do not know you, but you weep and and so do I, and surely that doth make us sisters in grief, and so because of that I'll follow you whither you list, and you will let me.

    CONSTANCE. Come then, and such cold comfort as I may
I'll share with you, but sorrow's cure is not
For us. Your lover groans in hell; my son,
My Arthur, lies within some oubliette,
Far down beneath the gracious day, dog's food
His only meat, and cries on me, his mother.

Then may I well make friends with stubborn grief,
Since grief alone the heavens have spar'd to me.

OPHELIA. Sad lady, I will go with you, weep
when you weep, and be your humble pensioner in
grief.

HAMLET [*advancing*] Ophelia, stay a little!
What! not know
Me yet? Doth recollection show thee naught
Familiar in these eyes, this face, this form?
What, faded quite, my love and me, from out
Thy memory as the summer shower when past
Is quick forgot with one short hour of sun?

OPHELIA. Love? I know what that doth signify. Is not love what we poor maids are fool'd
with? Thus have they told me, and therefore I'll
not listen to you, for indeed I never saw you before, that I remember, and yet there's something not
so strange lurks within your speech. But go your
ways, sweet sir. My Hamlet he is dead, and so I
care for none of mankind now. [*Sings*]

He is dead, perdy.

[*Exeunt* CONSTANCE *and* OPHELIA.
HAMLET. Alas, poor maid, I lov'd thee truly
once
And still had lov'd, and so had wedded thee

[ 17 ]

With all due rites, but that my father's ghost
Did stride between to part us evermore.

*[Sad music heard]*

*Exit* HAMLET *slowly.*

*Enter* LAUNCE *leading a dog.*

LAUNCE.   What a very dog is this my Crab here
'for a stony-hearted cur!   Why but now there met
us two distressed females weeping their hearts out
at their eyes, and sighing, moreover, as 'twould
move a very Turk to pity, and yet this cur took
no more note on 't than they had been two sticks
or stones.   Why, the Woman of Samaria would
have plucked out her hair in pity of the twain,
nay, so would I have done the same in her stead,—
yet what say I, for there's not so much hair on
my head as my mother's brass kettle has of its
cover.   A vengeance on 't, now where was I?   O,
truly, I was e'en at the Woman of Samaria.   Now,
good sirs, and gentles all, the Woman of Samaria had for ruth plucked out her hair, but
did not my dog Crab, who by your leaves is as
hairy a dog as goes on one-and-twenty toes, shed
even one hair in sorrow for the twain: not e'en the
smallest hair on 's nose.   And the matter of the
meeting was on this wise.   This small stone, with
the crack in 't, is the maid, she with the flowers; and

I think there be a crack in her wits, but no matter for that; this stone, a something bigger, ay, and with a crack in 't, too, shall be the lady with her hair all unbound; this tree shall be the dog; nay, that's not so neither, for I am the tree and the tree is me, and this stick is the dog, and thus it is. Now doth the small stone weep as 'twere a fountain gone astray, and may not speak for weeping; now doth the something bigger stone weep too, yet with a difference, and she doth not speak for weeping either, and truly I did weep likewise and no more could speak for my weeping than the poor distressed females might, yet there came all the while no word of comfort from this dog's mouth, not even one tear from his lids. Pray God, gentles all, there be no such hard hearts among any of you, or 'twere ten thousand pities. 'Tis an ill thing to have a sour nature like my dog Crab's, and no good comes on 't.

NURSE. Beshrew my heart, and that is so. My Mistress Juliet hath the tenderest and the most pitiful heart that lives in a maid's body, I do think, for she will weep by the hour together if she but behold a fly caught by the wings in a spider's web.

MERCUTIO [to ROMEO] No, Juliet, but a Niobe. Eh, man?

[ 19 ]

ROMEO.  Prate not of Juliet now, for I do love
Another way from her.

MERCUTIO.               O, Romeo,
Once yet again I tell thee; have a care!

*Enter* FALSTAFF.

FALSTAFF.  This were a goodly place enow, and
there were sack to be had.

TRINCULO [*aside*]  The fat fellow is verily in
the right on't, but since the old gentleman Prospero did give us here the sack there's no sack here
for the wishing.

FALSTAFF [*calls*]  Francis.

TRINCULO.  I think there be none here by that
name.

FALSTAFF.  'Tis no matter for the name;
the play 's the thing, the name is mere hollow-
ness and sound.  Here, you fellow with the dog,
you whoreson shaveling of a man, what is thy
name?

LAUNCE.  They call me Launce, an' it doth
please you, sir.

FALSTAFF.  How if I do not please?  Marry,
and what is *then* thy name?  Answer to that.

LAUNCE.  I could never i' the world tell that,
sir, and no more, indeed, sir, could my dog Crab

[ 20 ]

that's here, who, saving your presence, is the most hard-hearted cur alive. ⸱

FALSTAFF. No exceptions, good Launce; exceptions are the devil's counters, therefore, beware of exceptions. But hark you, good man Launce. Fetch me here some sack, and let it o'erflow the tankard, too, for I've a thirst upon me such as Hercules came most honestly by after his twelve labours.

LAUNCE. Please you, sir, I do not know the meanings of sack and Hercules. I did never see either of the gentlemen you speak of.

FALSTAFF. 'Tis no matter for Hercules, but, God's pity for 't, to be unacquainted with sack is to have lived as a dead man liveth. Sack, good Launce, is the prince of roystering blades; the pearl of price; the nonpareil of the world, the — nay, there's no fit comparison to be made. Ambrosia and nectar together were but ashes i' the mouth to 't.

TRINCULO [*coming forward*] You speak nothing aside the matter, sir, as I'm a true man. There's nought to be named i' the world before sack, and herein, of all places i' the world, there's no inn, no sack, no sack within. So you'll e'en have to stomach that, though you've small stomach to't.

FALSTAFF. Small stomach, say you? An' you denominate this belly of mine a small stomach, there's no truth in your tongue.

TRINCULO. And no sack in your stomach, either.

LAUNCE. These be as fine words as ever I heard.

FALSTAFF. Now, Sir Shaveling, and who bade you to speak?

LAUNCE. None, sir. I speak but when I have a mind, sir, and I am silent when I have a mind, likewise.

FALSTAFF. Have a mind to silence and let bigger men speak for you.

LAUNCE. Then I can tell who will do all the tongue-wagging, sir, for I spy none here that is bigger i' the girth than yourself.

FALSTAFF. As for the girth, Shaveling, that cometh of sack.

TRINCULO. And pillage of the larder, too, or I'm no true woman's son.

FALSTAFF. No inn within this heathen isle, no sack within the inn! Is this a fit place to bring a good Christian knight? 'T were enough to make a man of my sanguine and fiery composition turn

Muscovite on the instant, for your Muscovite, as I take it, is a most ungodly knave, and an infidel to boot, and without a moderate deal of sack, such as is needful for a man of my kidney, how is Christendom to be kept on its legs? What gives the justice discretion? Why, sack! What gives the lover whereby to gain the hand of his mistress? Why, sack! What gives the young man a merry heart and the old man a sanguine favour? Why, sack! What gives the soldier courage in the day of battle? Why, sack! Marry, then, he that hath his bellyful of sack hath discretion, courage, a ruddy visage, a merry heart and a nimble tongue.

LAUNCE [*aside*] The discretion that cometh with what he calls sack is e'en but a scurvy kind of discretion, to my thinking, for all of the stout gentleman's saying. Here's Crab, my dog, and he be not so niggard of his tongue, could tell so much as that comes to, on any day i' the week.

FALSTAFF. What be these folk that forswear sack? Why, lean anatomies with not so much blood in their bodies as would suffice for a flea's breakfast. The skin hangs upon their bones for all the world like a loose garment. You may feel the wind blow through their bodies. 'Twere a simple abuse of terms to call such starvelings men:

your poor forked radish would become the name
better.

MIRANDA.   This stout knight hath a nimble wit,
    in sooth,
But yet he doth not please me, for his eye
Bespeaks wanton desires, intemperate loves,
That ill do company his thin grey hairs.
   *Soft music heard.*
   [*Exeunt* FALSTAFF, LAUNCE, MERCUTIO,
     ROMEO, NURSE *and* PETER *by twos. A
     mist arises, and after a little vanishes.*

TRINCULO.   A murrain light on all unsociable
folk.   They might have bidden us to be of their
company, methinks.

STEPHANO.   Why, man, these are but ghosts
come from nowhere.   By the bones of my dead
grandsire, I've small mind to turn myself into a
ghost even thereby to leave this isle and Caliban's
hard service.   But, look you, Prospero's daughter
and her prince are stayed behind; an' they be not
ghosts of the same feather I marvel where they
have bestowed themselves on this isle since Prospero forsook it.

CALIBAN.   Will you be ever talking, fool?
   [*beats him*] take that,
And make your tongue a prisoner to your teeth.

STEPHANO *runs away, crying out loudly the while.*

*Enter the* FOOL *and* LEAR.

FOOL. Good nuncle, here be Christian folk; let's bide. The night cometh when a rotten thatch, even, is a more comfortable blanket than a skyful of little stars.

LEAR [*pointing to* MIRANDA] What, in Goneril's palace? Did she not with her own hands push her old father out of door? [*To* MIRANDA] Nay, mistress daughter; I'll not bide with you. A million murrains light upon thy unnatural head; ten million plagues burn in thy blood; a million million pains lurk in thy wretched bones, thou piece of painted earth whom 'twere foul shame to call a woman.

MIRANDA [*affrighted*] O Ferdinand, what
    means this strange old man?
There burns a direful lustre in his eye
And I do fear some certain harm from him.

FERDINAND. Sweet, do not so. He is but mad
    o'er some
Past wrong, and 'tis the quality of such
To take the true for false, and thus cry out
On him that's near, the guilty one not by.
See, he is faint and old, and cannot harm.

FOOL. Good nuncle, methinks the sun hath made of thee a very owl, for she whom thou callest upon so loudly is not so eld by twenty summers as thy daughter Goneril.

LEAR. 'Tis no matter for that. She is a woman and the daughter of a woman, therefore she will spin foul lies for her pleasure and bid her father out of sight when he is old.

FOOL. Fathers that give away all their substance ere they be dead and rotten are like to see strange things come to pass. An' thy bald crown had been worthy thy golden one it had worn thy golden one still and thou wert warm in thy palace.

LEAR. This daughter! O this daughter, Goneril.

*Enter* KING RICHARD II.

KING RICHARD. He lieth in his throat that
      swears I am
No king. 'Tis Bolingbroke doth wear the crown
He pluck'd from me, but there's no power can wash
Away a king's anointing. I put it by,
Being constrain'd, but that constraining told
Not of my will but my necessity.

FOOL. Lo! here's another wight that has given away his crown [*To* RICHARD] Art thou a king, too?

KING RICHARD. I am, and England was my
sovereignty.

FOOL. Then thou liest abominably, for a king
that lacks wit to keep his crown on 's head is no
king, and that's a true saying.

LEAR. Wert thou a king, indeed? Why so
was I.
And hadst thou daughters, black, unnatural?

KING RICHARD. Nor daughters nor no sons
have I to call
Me father.

LEAR. Then by so much art thou blest.
Forget not that, poor man that wast a king.

KING RICHARD. My kingdom was both daugh-
ter and my son,
And e'en as Judas sold his master Christ,
So did my kingdom chaffer for my crown,
And so deliver'd me to Bolingbroke.

FOOL. Is't he that hath thy crown?

KING RICHARD. 'Tis he, my sometime subject,
Bolingbroke:
He hath my crown and kingdom both, and I
Of all sad monarchs most disconsolate.

FOOL. Then have we here a pair of kings lack-
ing both crowns and kingdoms to wear 'em in.
These be but evil times for kings or fools either;

[ 27 ]

and to my thinking there's not so great a difference betwixt a fool and a king, save that the fool may chance be the wiser man of the two. Of a surety there was little wit a going begging when these twain put their golden crowns from off their simple skulls. Though I'm but a fool, and no wise man, I were but a fool indeed were I to change places with a king.

*Enter* KING HENRY VI.

KING HENRY. What sayest thou of kings?
        Kings are but men,
Cool'd by the same wind as their subjects are,
And blister'd by the self-same burning sun.
O happiest are the common folk who toil
Afield by day, eat scanty fare, and sleep
Anight unvex'd by cares of state or plots
Of traitorous nobles envious of a crown.

FOOL. What do I say of kings? Marry, I say they were best to watch well their daughters and their kingdoms; it needs no fool to say so much as that. Prithee, art thou a king of the same mould as these thou beholdest here in this place?

KING HENRY. At scarce nine months was I
        anointed king.

FOOL. Truly, thou serv'st a tender apprentice-

ship to thy business and I marvel the less at thy
present having. [*To* LEAR] Good nuncle, here's
yet another king out at the elbows, one, belike,
that shook his rattle as 't were a sceptre, and wore
his porringer on 's head where his crown should
have been.

    LEAR [*to* KING HENRY] And thou, too, wert
        a king?

    KING HENRY.         I was, but now
Am I a king no longer. Edward of March
Usurps my title and my crown. There come
No suitors unto me, a shadow prince
Mated with Madge of Anjou, strong where I
Am weak, for she loves war, and weak where I
Am strong, for I am joined to content
Which she, poor soul, wots little of.

    KING RICHARD.         O let
Us make a compact with this same content;
As which shall joy the most in it, that thus
The hours shall fleet unhinder'd o'er our heads
As o'er the shepherd's gazing on his flock
From out the hawthorn shade. Or what say you,
Were it not fitter pastime to bewail
Our loss of crown and kingdom morn by morn,
Evening by evening, till at last we died
Of grief?

KING HENRY.    Wiser it were to strive to find
What comfort's left to us.

KING RICHARD.            Why, so we will.
Come, fool, be thou our numbering clock and tell
Item by item all that's left to us
Unhappy kings, brothers in wretchedness.

LEAR.    A plague upon ye both that will not
    curse
The authors of your woes, that will not vex
The heavens with prayers for their undoing.
    Curse
On curse I'll heap upon the heads of those
She wolves, my daughters, sprung from out my
    loins;
The kingdom's ruin and their father's bane.

*[Exit raving.*

FOOL.    Farewell to you both, for I must after
him that's such an eager spendthrift of his
curses, and may each of you come upon a kingdom
to your mind — when the sun shall smite in Jan-
uary.                                    *[Exit* FOOL.

KING HENRY. A more than common grief
    look'd from his eye
That roll'd so wildly in his head; pray God
We keep our wits, whatever else be lost
To us.

KING RICHARD.. And I might see proud Boling-
broke
In such a case as his that parted now,
I deem that I could die full willingly.
    KING HENRY.  Would I were dead, an' it were
    God's good will;
But whilst I live I ne'er will còntrive aught
Of evil 'gainst mine enemy, nor wish
Him ill, for so weighs woe the heavier
On him invoking.  Our good captain Christ
Did bid us to the smiter turn the cheek
That's smitten yet again, nor harm him not
For all the mischiefs he doth put on us.
                    [*Soft music heard.*
    KING RICHARD.  How softly steals sweet music
    on the soul,
Shutting its doors to misery and pain,
Closing the senses 'gainst all foes without,
Turning the hard couch unto airy down,
Dissolving time in melting harmonies.
O I could list forever to its sound,
But it, or something stronger, masters me.
                            [*Sleeps.*
    KING HENRY.  Poor, changeful-hearted  man
    that wast a king,

Led captive by each wayward quick caprice,
Unhappy fate call'd thee unto a throne
As it did me; our kingdoms suffer'd for't.
Enjoy thy sleep by music underpropt,
Till waking show thee as thou wert before,
A crownless monarch weeping for thy crown.

[*Exit* KING HENRY.

MIRANDA. My heart is full of pity for these kings
Wanting their crowns.

FERDINAND. Those crowns had still been worn
Had they known truly what it is to be
A king. O, my Miranda, only such
That are compos'd of strength and gentleness
In fair proportion mix'd, should e'er essay
The sceptre. He that may not rule himself
Is of all monarchs least significant. [*Exeunt.*

## SCENE VI.

*A glade in another part of the island with* FERDINAND *and* MIRANDA *observed seated at the upper end thereof. Nearer at hand a group of Athenian citizens. Enter* BOTTOM, *wearing an ass's head.*

BOTTOM. Masters, you will marvel to behold

[ 32 ]

me here, but the very truth of the matter is that
I did fall asleep, and being asleep I did dream, and
as I did lie a-dreaming I was in a manner translated to this place, which methinks is an island, for
I did espy much water anear as I was brought
hither. But, masters, I do marvel much to look
upon you here also.

FRANCIS FLUTE. Methinks, friend Bottom, you
are not the sole wight in Athens esteemed worthy
translation.

ROBIN STARVELING. How an' we be not translated either?

PETER QUINCE. Robin Starveling speaks well
and to the centre of the matter. Know then, good
bully Bottom, we are translated as yourself, but
methinks you have lost more in the translating than
have we; is't not e'en so, masters all?

ALL. Right, good Peter Quince.

BOTTOM. I have lost nothing that should cause
you envy, good friends all, and so I assure you.
[Brays loudly] What say you then to my voice?
Is my voice perished?

TOM SNOUT. No, Nick Bottom.

BOTTOM. I thank you, good Tom Snout, and
to show you that I am the same Nick Bottom,
however my visage may appear altered, for travel

doth greatly age a man, as they say, you shall hear me wake the echoes once again.

*[Brays a second time, more loudly.*

QUINCE. Methinks your voice, good Bottom, has lost somewhat of sweetness.

BOTTOM. That's all one, good Peter Quince, for the simple truth of the matter is that you have no such delicate ear for fine harmonies as I am endow'd with. *[Strokes his ears.*

QUINCE. It doth seem so on more properer consideration, and I had an ear that were the parallax of yours 't were pity of my life.

ALL. Indeed, an' 'twere but pity of your life, Peter Quince.

BOTTOM. How say you, masters, shall not we spread ourselves? *[All sit down.*

MIRANDA. O Ferdinand, be these all mortal like Ourselves? More surely I did never spy So hideously strange a being such As he who hath the ass's head.

FERDINAND. Nor I. Belike he hath incurr'd some wizard's spite And, all unwitting, wears this semblance till The wizard's anger shall be spent. But see, His fellows play upon his ignorance

And of his strange beguilement make their sport.

BOTTOM. Since it is conceded by all of you
that I have lost nothing by translation, doth it not
follow, moreover, that I have somewhat gained by
that same adventure?

FLUTE. In good truth you have gained by
somewhat, Nick Bottom.

BOTTOM. I were an ass, indeed, an' I had not.

SNUG. And twice an ass, moreover, should he be
that would go about to steal it from you.

BOTTOM. Methinks that I could munch a sa-
voury salad of thistles with much stomach to't.

QUINCE. Your thistles be a thought too biting
for my stomach.

BOTTOM. 'Tis but likely. I was ever a choice
feeder. But, masters, was there not some matter
toward, or have you assembled yourselves but to
greet me, and, as 't were, fittingly?

QUINCE. You speak quite to the matter, good
Bottom. That is indeed the true end of our beginning. To behold your winsome visage in this
unwonted place is great joy to us simple mechan-
icals, yet we be nevertheless bold to proclaim to
you that to shave were not amiss to one of your
condition. For but bethink you, and you were

[ 35 ]

to come amongst ladies thus grievously beset with hair would shame us all.

SNUG. Mayhap in this strange part of the world 't would be thought matter for a hanging, and that were, indeed, a most serious business, to my thinking.

QUINCE. But an' we talk of ladies and hangings, moreover, hither comes a monstrous little lady, as 't were on the instant.

*Enter* TITANIA, *with her train.*

TITANIA. Where stays the gentle mortal I
    adore,
Whose voice unto mine ear makes harmonies
Celestial, and whose amiable face
Enthralls my heart in loving servitude?

PEASEBLOSSOM. Yonder he bides.

MOTH. 'Mong others of his kind.

COBWEB. Alike, yet different.

MUSTARDSEED.         Chief mortal seen.

TITANIA [*espying* BOTTOM] What angel can
    compare unto my love?
Beauty itself, beholding thee, might swoon
For envy, and the eldest sage would yield
His place to thee on th' instant. O my love!

         [*Winds her arms about his neck.*

Thou shalt dwell with me ever. Oberon
To thee is but a gaping pig, and thou
To him the nonpareil of beauteous youth.

BOTTOM. Good mistress atomy, though you
show somewhat spare of flesh you are yet of a
right comely countenance (and mine eyes do tell
me aught without spectacles), and you can speak
to the point upon occasion, as the present moment
doth signify most auspiciously.

TITANIA. O I could list unto thy silver tongue
Till Time itself wax'd eld and perished.

BOTTOM. How say you, masters? Hath not
mistress atomy a shrewd manner of observation an'
she singles me out from the company of my fellows
thus compellingly?

QUINCE. O bully Bottom, you are, as I take it,
the simple wonder of our age.

ALL. Right, master Quince. Nick Bottom is
become a very marvel.

TITANIA. Fain would I hear thy heavenly note
again.
Sing, wondrous mortal, while I link mine arms
About thy peerless form, or garlands twine
Of dewy flowers to hang about thy neck,
That neck, of all necks most incomparable.

BOTTOM [*sings*]

[ 37 ]

Upon the hay
Cophetua
Did waste the hours in sighing.
The beggar maid
Unto him said,
Good sir, are you a dying?

TITANIA.   That voice would make the night-
ingale asham'd.                         [*Kisses him*
Now must thou leave thy fellows in this place
And speed along with me unto my court,
Where we'll abide in loving dalliance
Until thy mortal part's with spirit mix'd.
Peaseblossom! Cobweb! Moth! and Mustardseed!
PEASEBLOSSOM.   Ready.
COBWEB.           And I.
MOTH.                   And I.
MUSTARDSEED.              And I.
ALL.                         Your hest,
Our queen, is still our duty and delight.
TITANIA.   Attend us to the court, and evermore
Give special heed unto this gentleman,
Anticipate his ev'ry wish and feed
Him with the choicest cates the isle doth yield.

*Exeunt* TITANIA *and* BOTTOM, *attended by
train.*

QUINCE. Were this but told in Athens, now, 't were not believed by aught, but we accredited liars all of the first water, and so esteemed.

ALL. 'T were indeed but so, and truly, Peter Quince.

QUINCE. Therefore I hold that (an' we once more come by our own firesides in Athens), we were best make no words of the happenings we have beheld but now, lest we be cried upon in the public streets as those that be counted no true men.

ALL. That were to shame us, every mother's son.

QUINCE. Why you speak the very gizzard of the matter, my masters all, and we will be silent in such wise as I did perpetuate, and as for Nick Bottom, let his goblin mistress do with him as she listeth, for methinks we are well rid of his company, being, for ourselves, nothing loose-minded but sober, virtuous citizens all.

ALL. That are we, Peter Quince, and we thank God for't.

*Enter* PUCK, *unperceived, who tweaks* QUINCE *violently by the nose and exit.*

QUINCE. O masters, which of you —

*Is suddenly twitched aside by* PUCK. *Re-enters with a lion's head on his shoulders.*

[ 39 ]

ALL. God defends us, Peter Quince.

QUINCE. Masters, it ill becomes you as sober citizens of Athens to treat one of yourselves thus unseemly. Am not I a simple workman like the rest of you? Is it not my very own voice that you hear but now? [*Roars.*

ALL. God for his mercy.

[*Exeunt all but* QUINCE.

QUINCE. These be strange manners; an' I were a very lion, though being of a truth of a most lamblike perdition, they could not have fled from me with greater speeding. I will e'en after them to taste the reason of their knavery.

### *Enter* PUCK.

PUCK. Now will I set these patches by the ears,
Making such monsters of their simple selves
As severally shall fright them when they see
Each in the other's fearful eyeball glass'd.

[*Exit* PUCK.

### *Re-enter* QUINCE.

QUINCE. And I can spy but one of my neighhours in this predestinated place I'll be hanged.

*Re-enter* STARVELING, *with an owl's head.*

QUINCE. Bless us, Robin Starveling, what wizardry do I spy in you?

STARVELING. Wizardry, an' you call it, Peter Quince? Look to your own head an' you would find out wizardry. There's naught strange in me.

*Re-enter* SNUG, *with a bear's head.*

QUINCE *and* STARVELING. Save us, good Snug, how art thou transmogrified!

SNUG. Not so, neither, neighbours both. I am but Snug the joiner, as you might behold him of any working day, but you twain, methinks, are most marvellously encountered.

QUINCE *and* STARVELING. Speak for yourself, Master Snug: we are the same as you have known us ever.

QUINCE. That is, I am the same, but Master Starveling is quite other than the simple man he was.

STARVELING. Thou liest, Peter Quince. I am but plain Robin Starveling, but you are become a very monster.

*Re-enter* SNOUT, *with a deer's head and horns.*

QUINCE. Good masters three, you are enchanted, and pity o' my life it is. 'Tis I alone that doth remain as much mankind as I was ever.

SNOUT. An' you count yourself the proper likeness of a man you are most horribly mistook, and so it is, Peter Quince.

[ 41 ]

*Re-enter* FLUTE, *with the head of a crocodile.*

FLUTE.   O neighbours all, what behold I here?
What sorcerer has thus exorcised upon you?   O
could you be spy upon yourselves to know how un-
like you are to plain citizens like me.

QUINCE.   A plain man, say you.   Forsooth,
yours is a very fearful manner of plainness, Francis Flute.   But look at me, masters all, and you
would gaze upon a plain man.

STARVELING.   Nay, look on me, in his stead.

SNOUT.   Not so, but on me.

SNUG.   These be liars, every mother's son.
Look upon me, I say, Francis Flute.

FLUTE.   Masters, hear but the simple truth.
You are all of you deceived and have suffered most
horrible enchantment, every mother's son of you
but me.   Heaven help you, neighbours, and undo
the spell that each and every one may become as I
am.                         [*Gnashes his jaws fearfully.*

ALL.   That were most dire affliction of any that
be in the varsal world, Francis Flute.

FLUTE.   And you were not something other
than simple mankind I could try conclusions with
you that speak thus enviously.   Indeed, I am
something that way toward, but now.

                    [*Exeunt Omnes, fighting.*

*Enter* Puck.

Puck. Thus have I put the simple senses all
Of these rude knaves sorely distraught, for each
Doth fear the other, deeming him the prey
Of dark enchantment, while himself believes
Himself none other than he was at first

Lord, how simple mortals be,
And it much doth pleasure me
To behold them all distraught;
Each in fairy toils is caught,
There to bide at my good will,
Roaring, growling, fighting still.

[*Exit* Puck.

Ferdinand. How like you this, Miranda?
Hath not he,
The gamesome elf, made merry mischief so
'Mongst these dull wits that scarce may they once
more
Regain their sometime selves and liberty.
Miranda. 'Twas merry, sooth, yet I could
wish the spell
Dissolv'd that made them fearsome to themselves,
And enemies that once were friends. He that
Hath friends hath treasure, more than wealth of
Ind,

[ 43 ]

And he that hath not still is poor indeed,
Though all the gold of Ophir 'long'd to him.
*Enter* JAQUES, *laughing.*
JAQUES.   Though I be sworn to sadness it doth
make
Me gladsome 'gainst my disposition
To note the antics of these greasy fools
Of Athens, pent within the glade where I,
All unobserv'd, have play'd the spy upon
'Em this full hour.   How like these fustian churls
Be to their fellows of the scepter'd throne,
The ermine robe, the 'broider'd chasuble.
'Tis habit makes the man, the wearer's naught.
The fool, when he is naked, shows as sage
As the philosopher so furnished;
The lout's bare hide's no worser than the king's,
And, when their pride is fondly touch'd, all men
Are brothers.   Did not each Athenian wight
Beholding all his fellows in their guise
Most strange and horrible, yet deem himself
Perch'd high above the reach of wizardry,
And sole possessor of a countenance
Such as is worn 'mongst ordinary folk?
My sides do ache with mirth when I bethink
Me of these simple churls, and of their kin
By Adam, in high places set, how each,

No matter what his state, doth ne'er perceive
Himself glass'd in his fellow's eye, but paints
Instead a portrait in fair colours mix'd,
Calls it his likeness, and would have the world,
That knows him what he is, declare its truth
Both in the general and particular.
This globe is peopl'd with philosophers
And fools, methinks, by which I mean the wise
Are the sole wearers of the motley coat
And all men else do owe the cap and bells.
The lover is a fool who doth proclaim
His mistress is perfection; the maid,
Who thinks her swain compact of truth; the king,
Who stakes his crown upon a battle's point;
The soldier, who for glory gives his life
And dies, a forfeit to't; the tonsur'd saint,
Who vows to heaven that which 'longs to men.
O, I could moralize upon this theme
An hour by the clock, with still grave matter left
For melancholy contemplation.     [*Exit* JAQUES.
    MIRANDA.   Yon sober suited wight, meseems,
        doth make
A play of sadness.
    FERDINAND.        So, in sooth, he doth.
His wisdom rings but hollowly, and all
His speech declares a studied wilfulness

Such as we note in him who acts a part
That finds no smallest likeness in himself.
*Soft music heard, followed by a dance of elves.*
*[Exeunt* FERDINAND *and* MIRANDA.

## SCENE VII.

*Still another part of the island.*

*Enter* PROSPERO.

PROSPERO.  Now have I 'complish'd that I did
　　intend,—
Dispers'd Miranda's sadness utterly,
And, for a brief space, made the airy dreams
Of Master Shakescene take on form again
As erst in other lands and climes, that so
These married lovers might be entertain'd
Full pleasingly, and gather from the hours
Spent in this isle of summer, honey'd sweets
For fond remembrance in the tide of time.
My Ariel!  What, Ariel, I say!　*[Enter* ARIEL.
Thanks, gentle Ariel, who hast again
Done all my bidding.  But for thee my art
Had halted ere its best.  Once more receive
My thanks, who am much bound to thee.
ARIEL.　　　　　　　　　　　This time,
Good master Prospero, I serv'd for love

Not duty, and I count your thanks reward
In fullest measure. And there be nothing else
You would of me, then, Prospero, adieu.
    PROSPERO. Adieu, gentlest of spirits, Ariel.
                              [*Exit* ARIEL.
    *Thunder heard and* PROSPERO *vanishes.*


## SCENE VIII.

*A room in the palace at Naples.*

    *Enter* FERDINAND *and* MIRANDA.

MIRANDA. O Ferdinand, my love, last night I
    slept
And sleeping dream'd, and in my dream I saw
The isle where first you knew me, where we told
Each to the other our fond loves. Methought
I was by you companion'd and the hours
Did move to music while there pass'd before
Our wond'ring eyes, as for our sole delight,
A many folk, strange sorted, who did talk
Together, and at whiles as 'twere a play
And we beholding it. 'Twas wondrous strange.
    FERDINAND. O, my Miranda, sure some power
    we wot
Not of doth play with us as we at chess
Do move the pieces this way first and that,

Because our will is to't.    Know then that I
Did dream the fellow unto yours (if it
In very truth were that and nothing more).
Like you, I vis'ted that sweet spot, with you
Beside the while, and did behold, as on
A stage a company of players strut
Their hour or two, a band of merry folk
With some that wept and cried out upon fate.
Who knoweth, my Miranda, what doth hap
To us when we do sleep?    At whiles we note
In slumber tokens of a life apart
From this, alike, yet not alike, and who
May say how far the spirit wanders when
The body sleeps?

    MIRANDA.        Would all my dreams were like
To this we've wak'd from, for 'twas sweet, yet sad,
And not so sad but that 'twas sweet the more.
I would it were to dream again.

    FERDINAND.             Who knows,
Sweet Saint Miranda, but it will return?

          *Soft music again heard.*
            [*Exeunt* FERDINAND *and* MIRANDA.

# II

# THE MERCHANT OF VENICE:

# ACT SIXTH

# THE MERCHANT OF VENICE:
## ACT SIXTH

### Scene I.

*Venice. A street.*

*Enter* Shylock, *followed by a rabble of
shouting citizens.*

First Citizen. Shylock, how speeds thy busi-
ness at the court?
Where is the pound of flesh thou covetest?
Second Citizen. How likest thou the judge
from Padua?
Third Citizen. Eh, Jew, an upright judge!
thou hast my lord
The duke to thank for thy poor life. Had I
But been thy judge a halter had been thine,
And thou had'st swung in't, yet, beshrew my life,
'Twere pity that good Christian hemp were
stretch'd
To hang a misbegotten knave like thee.

[ 51 ]

FOURTH CITIZEN.  Shylock, thou infidel, thou
  should'st have had
The lash on thine old back ten score of times
Ere they had suffer'd thee from out the court.
  FIFTH CITIZEN.  A beating shall he have, e'en
  now, the knave.          [*Beats* SHYLOCK.
SHYLOCK [*striking about him angrily*]  Aye!
  kill me, dogs of Christians, an' ye will!
Meseems the Jew hath no more leave to tread
The stones on Christian streets; he may not breathe
The air a Christian breathes, nor gaze uncheck'd
Upon the Christian's sky; he hath no part
Or lot in anything that is, unless
A Christian please to nod the head.  I hate
Ye, brood of Satan that ye are!  May all
The plagues of Egypt fall upon ye, dogs
Of Christians; all the pains —
  FOURTH CITIZEN.          Nay, gentle Jew,
'Tis said thou must become a Christian, straight;
Old Shylock, turn perforce, a " Christian dog!"
Now, greybeard infidel, how lik'st thou this?
  SHYLOCK.  Eternal torments blister him that
  asks.

          [*Exit* SHYLOCK, *raving.*

[ 52 ]

SECOND CITIZEN. A sweet-fac'd Christian will
our Shylock make.
I would that I might be his cònfessor,
To lay such swingeing penance on the knave
As scarce would leave him space to sup his broth
Amid the pauses of his punishment.

*[Exeunt citizens, with shouts.*

## SCENE II.

*Venice. A Room in* SHYLOCK'S *House.*

*Enter* SHYLOCK *and* TUBAL.

TUBAL. How now, Shylock! What bitter woe
looks from thy face? What has chanced to thee
in the Christian's court to make thee thus distraught?

SHYLOCK. O Tubal, Tubal, there dwells no
more pity in the Christian breast than there abides
justice therein. I stood for justice and mine own,
before them all; before that smiling, smooth-faced
judge from Padua, and with those false smiles of
his he turned against me the sharp edge of the
law. He forbade the shedding of one drop of the
merchant Antonio's blood — naming therefor some
ancient law, musty for centuries, and that still had

[ 53 ]

gathered dust till it would serve to bait the Jew with — and so I lost my revenge upon Antonio. More than that, good Tubal, I lost everything I had to lose.

TUBAL. Lost everything! Now, by our ancient prophets, this is woe indeed.

SHYLOCK. Aye, good Tubal. The half my goods are now adjudged Antonio's; the other half, upon my death, goes to the knave, Lorenzo; that same he that lately stole my ducats and my daughter.

TUBAL. And merry havoc will he and thy daughter Jessica make of thy treasure, Shylock.

SHYLOCK. But there is greater woe to come, good Tubal. To save this poor remainder of a life have I this day sworn to turn a Christian.

TUBAL. Thou, turn Christian! O monstrous deed! Our synagogue will be put to everlasting shame for this. Nay, good Shylock, it must not be. It must not be.

SHYLOCK. Have I not said that I am sworn on pain of life? They would e'en have had my life almost in the open court had I not so sworn. But hear me, Tubal; I will not die till that I have bethought me of some secret, sure revenge upon Antonio, or failing this, upon the taunting, sneer-

ing fool they call Gratiano, whom I do loathe e'en
as I loathe Antonio. Moreover I would gladly do
some deadly hurt unto the accursed Paduan judge,
an' it might be so.

TUBAL. Then wilt thou still be Hebrew at the
heart, good Shylock?

SHYLOCK. How else while yet I bear remembrance of my wrongs? Have not many of our
chosen people done this selfsame thing for ducats
or for life? Kissed the cross before men's eyes,
but spurned it behind their backs? As I shall do,
erewhile. But, O good Tubal, the apples of
Sodom were as sweet morsels in the mouth unto this
that I must do.

TUBAL. Hebrew at heart, albeit Christian of
   countenance.
Ay, Shylock, it is well. It is well.　　　[*Exeunt.*

## SCENE III.

*Venice. Interior of Saint Mark's.*

*Organ music heard. Enter a company of noble
   Venetians with the* DUKE *and his train, ac-
   companied by* BASSANIO, PORTIA, ANTONIO,
   GRATIANO, NERISSA *and others. Following
   these, at a little distance, appear* LORENZO

*and* JESSICA, *the latter gorgeously attired,*
*The company pauses before the font.* SHY-
LOCK *enters from the left, led forward by a*
*priest. His gaberdine has been exchanged*
*for the Christian habit, and in his hand is*
*placed a crucifix.*

DUKE.  Old Shylock, art thou well content to do
As thus we have ordain'd, which is, that thou
Renounce thine ancient Jewish faith, repent
Thy sins, and take the holy, solemn vows
A Christian takes when on his brow the drops
Baptismal glister, and be nam'd anew
After the Christian custom of our land?

SHYLOCK.  Most noble duke, I am content, and
     do
Hereby renounce my nation and my faith,
And, which is more, raze out of mind the name
That I have borne these three-score heavy years,
Since it is thy command.

DUKE.            Cristofero
Shalt thou be call'd hereafter.  Now, good priest,
Thine office do with ceremonies meet,
And make this greybeard Jew a Christian straight.

    *Solemn music heard, after which* SHYLOCK *is*
       *baptized by the priest,* ANTONIO *at the*
       *command of the* DUKE *standing godfather*

*to the Jew, who makes the required re-
sponses in a low voice. While he is still
kneeling the company converse in an under-
tone.*

GRATIANO.  I much mislike this new made Chris-
tian's face
Nor would I trust Cristofero for all
His Christian name and meekly mutter'd vows.
PORTIA.  Nay, Gratiano, question not the heart
Nor rudely draw aside the veil that speech
Hangs ever 'fore the spirit.  Who may say
That e'en the best among us keeps a faith
Loyal to every smallest clause, or does
Not slip at whiles amid the thousand small
Requirements of the law.  And yet, we do
Implore a gentle sentence on these sins
Of ours, a pardon that shall make us whole.
If, for ourselves, then trebly for the Jew
New come, bewilder'd, to our Christian creed.
ANTONIO.  There will be space enow to doubt
the Jew
Turn'd Christian, Gratiano, when he shall
Give cause for doubt.  'T were scantest charity
Till then, to bear with him, as we do bear
Ourselves unto our fellow Christians all.
A bitter lesson hath he lately conn'd,

And he were mad indeed that should neglect
To profit by't.

GRATIANO.    Belike, belike 'tis thus,
But yet I do not like Cristofero's looks;
I'll not be argu'd out of that, i' faith,
And say't again, I much mislike his favour.

NERISSA.    Peace, Gratiano, dost not note the
        duke
Commands to silence, and would speak once more?
Thou wilt be ever talking, as thy wont.

DUKE.    Cristofero, thou bear'st a Christian
        name
From this day forth.    Then look to't that thou
        dost
In all things as a Christian, not as Jew.

SHYLOCK.    In all things as a Christian.    Yes.
        [*Aside*]    Why that's
Revenge! Revenge!

DUKE.                So must thou quit thy house
In Jewry, dwell mid Christian folk, and go
With Christian folk to church on holy days,
And wear henceforth the cross thou did'st disdain.
Dost hearken unto us, Cristofero?

SHYLOCK.    I hear but to obey, dread duke; and
        thank
Thee for thy clemency to me, once Jew,

But now, within this very selfsame hour,
A gasping new born Christian, all unschool'd
In duties other Christians know full well,
Yet earnest still, to act the Christian's part,
With hope to better his ensample set.

GRATIANO [*aside to* BASSANIO] For all thy
gentle Portia saith but now,
I like not such smooth terms from out those lips.

BASSANIO [*aside*] Peace, Gratiano, let him say
his say,
He cannot now do aught to injure thee.
[*Exeunt* DUKE *and train with* ANTONIO *and
friends.* LORENZO *and* JESSICA *come forward.*

JESSICA. How now, good father Cristofero;
what a pair of Christians are we both. Only
there's this difference betwixt us, good father. I
am a Christian for love of a husband and you have
turned a Christian for love of your ducats.

SHYLOCK. Ungrateful daughter; Why did'st
thou go forth from my house by night and rob thy
grey-haired father of his treasure?

JESSICA. Why? That's most easy of answer.
Why, because I desired a Christian husband and
there was no coming by my desire save by secret
flight from your most gloomy chambers; and since

neither my Christian husband nor your daughter Jessica could by any kind of contriving live upon air alone, we had, perforce, to take with us some of your ducats for the bettering our condition. Speak thou for me, Lorenzo. Was it not e'en so?

LORENZO. Old man, I am sorry for that I was forced to take from you your daughter and your ducats against your good pleasure, but I must tell you that I loved her as myself [*Aside*] nay, much more, my Jessica,— and by reason of this great love of mine, and because of your exceeding hatred towards all Christians did I take her from your house. And since, moreover, as the maid very truly says, there's no living i' the world without the means to live, because of this did we make shift to take with us from your house such means, as well advised you would not have your daughter lack for food and suitable apparel, and since we are now Christians all, what matters it?

SHYLOCK [*slowly*] Ay, what matters it? We are now Christians all, as thou sayest, and, I remember me that I have heard it said it is a Christian's duty to forgive all who have wronged him. Therefore I forgive you, Jessica — for robbing your old father; and you, Lorenzo, I forgive — for stealing my daughter. You are each well

mated.  But I would be alone a while.  Go, good
Jessica.  Go, son Lorenzo.

> [*Exeunt* LORENZO *and* JESSICA.

SHYLOCK [*alone*]  A curse pursue the twain
  where'er they go.
A Christian-Jewish curse, since that should be
Weightier than either singly.  Would that I
Might see them dead before me, while I live,—
Such love I bear my daughter, and my son.

> [*Gazes about the church.*

These be the images of Christian saints
Whom I must bend the knee before when men
Look on.  And here the Virgin; here the Christ.
Now must I kneel; a hundred eyes perchance,
Peer at me through the gloom.  A hundred eyes
May see me kneel, yet shall they not perceive
The scorner of the Christian hid within
The humble figure of the man who kneels.
Now, by the prophets, whom I reverence,
And by these Christian saints whom I do scorn,
I swear to nourish my revenge till those
I deepest hate are dead, or sham'd before
Their fellows.  But how this may be, I know
Not yet, for all the way were dark as night
Before me, save that my revenge burns red.

> [*Choir heard chanting in a distant chapel.*

[*Rises from his knees.*

Good fellow Christians, it may hap the Jew
Turn'd Christian, shall yet do a harm to ye.
Behind Cristofero's mask is still the face
Of Shylock; in his breast the heart unchang'd.

[*Choir heard chanting* Judica me Deus.

Yea, my good fellow Christians, I do thank
Ye for that word, and hug it to my heart.
Henceforth it shall be mine, when I do pray,
Not to thy Christ, but unto Israel's God!
" Give sentence with me, O my God; defend
My cause against the hosts that wrought me ill."

[*Choir in the distance, responding* Amen.
*Exit* SHYLOCK.

# NOTE BY WILLIAM J. ROLFE, Litt.D.

It is a tribute of no slight significance to Shakespeare's skill in the delineation of character that we instinctively regard the personages in his mimic world as real men and women, and are not satisfied to think of them only as they appear on the stage. We like to follow them after they have left the scene, and to speculate concerning their subsequent history. The commentators on *Much Ado*, for instance, are not willing to dismiss Benedick and Beatrice when the play closes without discussing the question whether they probably " lived happily ever after." Some, like Mrs. Jameson and the poet Campbell, have their misgivings about the future of the pair, fearing that " poor Benedick " will not escape the " predestinate scratched face " which he himself had predicted for the man who should woo and win that " infernal Até in good apparel," as he called her; while others, like Verplanck, Charles Cowden-Clarke, Furnivall, and Gervinus, believe that their married life will be of " the brightest and sunniest."

Some have gone back of the beginning of the plays, like Mrs. Cowden-Clarke in her *Girlhood of Shakespeare's Heroines*, and Lady Martin (Helena Faucit) in her paper on Ophelia in *Some of Shakespeare's Female Characters*.

[ 68 ]

Others, like Mr. Adams, have made the experiment of continuing a play of Shakespeare in dramatic form. Ernest Renan, in France, and Mr. C. P. Cranch, in this country, have both done this in the case of *The Tempest*, mainly with the view of following out the possible adventures of Caliban after Prospero had left him to his own devices.

These and similar sequels to the plays are nowise meant as attempts to " improve " Shakespeare (like Nahum Tate's version of *Lear*, that held the stage for a hundred and sixty years) and sundry other perversions of the plays in the eighteenth century, which have damned their presumptuous authors to everlasting infamy. They are what Renan, in his preface, calls his *Caliban*,—" an idealist's fancy sketch, a simple fantasy of the imagination."

Mr. Adams's Sixth Act of *The Merchant of Venice* is an experiment of the same kind; not, as certain captious critics have regarded it, a foolhardy attempt to rival Shakespeare. It was originally written for an evening entertainment of the " Old Cambridge Shakespeare Association." No one in that cultivated company misunderstood the author's aim, and all heartily enjoyed it. I believe that it will give no less pleasure to the larger audience to whom it is now presented in print.